the farm

All inquiries should be addressed to:
Barron's Educational Series, Inc.
250 Wireless Boulevard
Hauppauge, New York 11788

Library of Congress Catalog Card No. 91-8755

International Standard Book No. 0-8120-4711-7

Library of Congress Cataloging-in-Publication Data
Sánchez, Isidro.
   [Huerto.   English]
   The farm / I. Sánchez, C. Peris. — 1st ed.
      p.   cm. — (Discovering nature)
   Translation of: El huerto.
   Summary: Explains how vegetables are grown on a farm. Includes information for parents and teachers.
   ISBN 0-8120-4711-7
   1. Farms—Juvenile literature.   2. Truck farming—Juvenile literature.   3. Vegetables—Juvenile literature.   4. Agriculture—Juvenile literature.   [1. Farms.   2. Vegetables.]   I. Peris, C. (Carme).
II. Title.   III. Series: Sánchez, I. (Isidro).   Discovering nature.
S519.R5813   1991
635—dc20

                      91-8755
                      CIP
                      AC

Legal Deposit: B. 14.945-91
Printed in Spain
1234   987654321

discovering nature

the farm

I. Sánchez

C. Peris

BARRON'S

New York • Toronto • Sydney

Today is the first day of our vacation at our grandparents' farm.

We have fresh vegetables for lunch. All of them were picked this morning!

To work on the farm, we must understand how plants grow. We must also know how t use hoes and other tools.

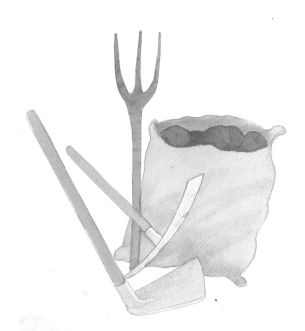

My grandfather grows many different kinds of vegetables.

Lettuce is used in salads. Cauliflower is good cooked or raw.

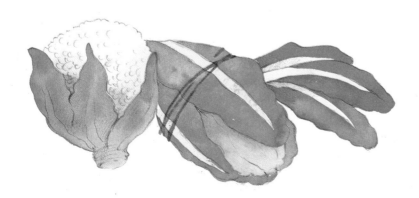

Rabbits love carrots. Sometimes they get to eat them before we do!

Tomato plants grow on vines that are tied to stakes. The vines grow high and full of juicy red tomatoes.

Peas and beans also grow on vines that are tied to stakes. Instead of a sprinkler, my grandfather has dug narrow ditches to bring them water.

We can't see potatoes while they are growing because they are underground. But their healthy green leaves tell us where they are!

In the greenhouse the seeds are planted in flat boxes. When they sprout, the young plants are moved outside.

Today we are going to the market with Grandfather to sell our vegetables.

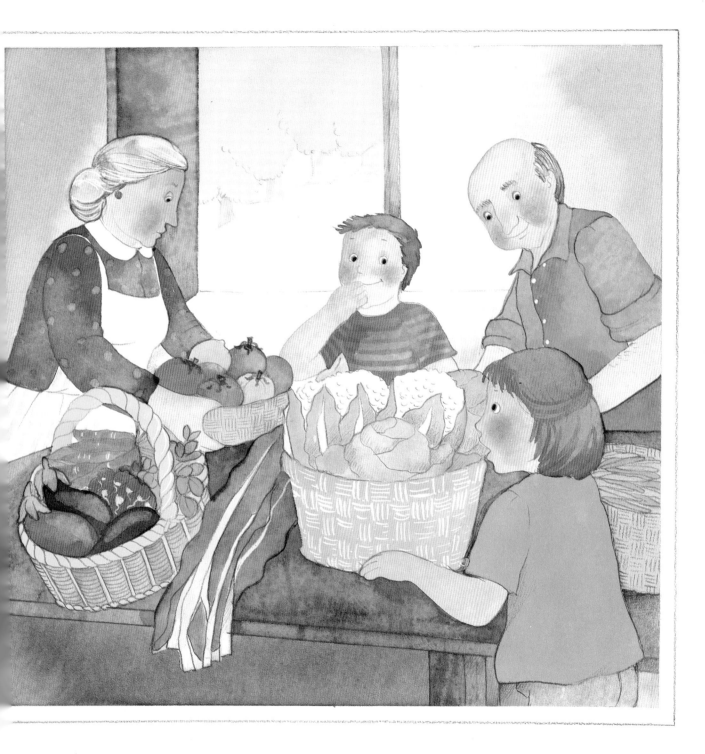

At the market we see other
farmers who are selling
their products.

The vegetables our grandparents grow on their farm are very tasty. They are also very good for all of us!

THE FARM

City and country

City people rarely, if ever, see farm products in their natural and original state. Fruit, vegetables, poultry, etc. are usually only available in plastic bags on the shelves or frozen food sections of stores and supermarkets.

While frozen food is convenient, it provides city-dwellers with an image of food products that has little to do with their natural look and taste. If this is true for adults, it is even truer for children. For many city youngsters, for example, peas are simply little green balls that come out of the freezer in plastic bags or cardboard boxes.

It may eventually come to pass that our children will find it difficult to believe that the plucked, shrink-wrapped product we call "chicken" once had feathers! Life in the city has made its inhabitants lose any sense of a very important aspect of civilization—agriculture and the role of the farmer.

Providing children with an understanding of agriculture is an important and pleasant task that can start with a visit to a nearby farm, or with the cultivation of a small vegetable garden at home or at school.

The teacher is at an advantage because products from the vegetable garden are seasonal. Their cycles begin and end at certain times of the year. For example, there is a time for planting beans and another for cabbage, a time for picking tomatoes, and another for pumpkins. Thus, from early spring until late fall, children can plant, grow, and then pick different vegetables and have the satisfaction of taking them home to enjoy while they are really fresh.

The importance of vegetables

With the teacher's help, children can begin to understand why we raise cattle and grow vegetables. They should be taught that many substances important for their development come from vegetables: carbohydrates, protein, oils, vitamins, fiber, etc. By observing the vegetable garden and working in it, children will learn to appreciate its importance (and that of the farmers who work it) in providing the necessary elements to help us grow and develop. They will understand that the meat they eat would not be available if pastures did not produce enough grass and fodder (alfalfa, barley, corn, etc.) to nourish the cattle. The earth supplies the vegetables to feed herbivorous animals and, thanks to these animals, we have the meat we need.

The importance of the soil

We live on soil and from soil. Children who come into contact with nature through school or at home can quickly distinguish between "playing" with the soil and "working" the soil.

The teacher can show the child that the latter is a very important activity that consists of preparing the fields for the vegetables to grow. "Working" the soil means:

- loosening the soil by plowing or digging;
- fertilizing it to provide nitrogen and minerals; and
- watering it regularly.

Love of the earth is taught simply and effectively by harvesting and enjoying the vegetables that the child has helped to grow.